BENEATH THE MOONLIGHT

by Rick McQuiston

Edited by Rick and Rosemary McQuiston.

Cover concept and artwork by Rick McQuiston.

Website: many-midnights.webs.com

Email: Many_Midnights@yahoo.com

Dedicated to my family.

ISBN# 978-1-105-62598-5

Welcome.

Here are some of my latest trips into the darkest regions of my mind. I hope you enjoy them.

There's demons infesting dreams, killer cars, haunted roads, cemeteries, and that thing we all fear the most: Time itself (although in my tale it isn't growing old that you'll be afraid of).

So please, light another blood-red candle, pour a hot cauldron of tea, and be careful when you tread Beneath the Moonlight.

CONTENTS

Mr. Nightmare   1

Arden Bluff   7

All That Remains   17

Time   23

Hunger   27

The Depth of Things   33

A Tense Situation   37

A Part of Cars Forever   41

Appearances   47

Stepping Stones   55

An Old Neglected Cemetery   61

Imagination   67

MR. NIGHTMARE

Melody knew it would be there, it simply had to be.
It had to be there. It had to be there.

The sounds that echoed in the house were as predictable as they were frightening. They were the same noises that she had endured so many times before, at least 10 by her count, but they still got under her skin just the same.

And she knew why...all too well.

Mr. Nightmare.

The man, or whatever it was, was always right behind the sounds, as if he held them on a string, periodically tossing them out in front of him like a fisherman casting out a line in search of the perfect bass. Melody knew what his, or its, technique was. She had lived through it before.

She glanced at the puppy dog clock that hung on the far wall in the dining room. The comfort it offered, a trip back to happier times, appealed to her, despite their empty promises of safety. She loved that clock even though it was a rather gaudy timepiece that hardly looked good anywhere in the house. But her parents had given in to their little girl's desires and hung it in the house for all to see.

A bead of sweat trickled down her forehead and settled in her left eye, causing a slight stinging sensation. She was tempted to wipe it away before it
reached her eye but that would mean deviation from the norm, something Mr. Nightmare looked for, and attempted to exploit.

The puppy dog clock showed the time as its monotonous ticks bore into Melody's already frail nerves.

10:15 p.m.

It was the same every time.

10:15 p.m.

It was the dreaded time when Mr. Nightmare started his ominous stroll towards her.

10:15 p.m. The beginning of the end.

The footsteps resonated in her ears, further heightening the tension in the air. He was coming for her just like before. Just like all the other times.

She briefly entertained the prospect of running up to him, of facing her fears head on. Perhaps he would back down when confronted with such a bold and unsuspected move.

But then a memory of what he looked like quickly dispelled the notion. And besides she didn't do that the first time, or the second, or the third. The consequences that would probably occur if she did anything differently were not something she cared to endure.

Once, she had discovered what could happen if she did anything differently. Something like the Butterfly Effect, she surmised. Any change in the past, however small or insignificant, could alter the future, often with disastrous results.

In her unique case however it was the present that could alter the future…her future, if she even had one.

Once, she had simply wiped away sweat from her eyes. That small seemingly inconsequential action allowed Mr. Nightmare to nearly overtake her. By taking her eyes off of her surroundings he was able to slither up to her, ready to strike.

Pale moonlight slipped into the house anywhere it could. It was the only illumination there was, hardly providing enough light to see where one is walking, much less for someone looking for a particular item.

But it did cast enough light directly on the puppy dog clock, clearly showing the time. Apparently she was meant to be aware of the time.

The footsteps were gradually increasing in speed and depth. Mr. Nightmare was all too aware of the psychological effect his 'calling cards' had on his intended victim, and he used them as a weapon, further weakening the prey's strength.

Melody knew what she had to do next. It was pointless and futile, but she had no choice. She ran over to the front door and twisted the knob.

Nothing.

She picked up the silver candlestick holder she had given to her mother as a birthday gift and slammed it into a nearby window.

Nothing.

She kicked the door with all of her might and hit it with the candlestick holder as hard as she could.

Nothing.

The puppy dog clock showed 10:17 p.m. Mr. Nightmare was getting closer. It would only be another four minutes until the part Melody hated the most happened...he made his appearance at the end of the hall.

She wanted to cry, to give in to the submissive urge. She wanted to collapse where she stood. She wanted to end it all, regardless of what would happen to her. But the fact that she held the power to defeat Mr. Nightmare spurred her on. She knew very well what she had to do; she only needed to wait for the appropriate time.

The cold moonlight cast its glow on most of the floor and walls of the hallway. Mr. Nightmare stood near the basement door at the end of the hallway. He was safely within the confines of the darkness, wrapping himself up in it like a toddler in his favorite blanket.

Melody steadied her nerves. She wanted to look away, to spare herself from the torture of seeing the creature yet again, but she couldn't do that. She must face her fears and overcome them. The first time, she had stared into its face and saw the evil hunger in its numerous eyes. She saw the nauseating ooze dripping from its oversize mouth and its tightened claws encrusted with the dirt of a thousand graves. She witnessed the monstrosity that tormented her soul beyond comprehension, and yet felt the need to look at it. It completed her in some twisted way.

Mr. Nightmare leaned forward, barely touching the deadly moonlight, being cautious to avoid it as much as possible. He knew he had to reveal some of his features to the human, but only enough to increase her fear and loathing.

3

The moonlight singed his pallid flesh, causing him to recoil in pain. The human had seen his features though; her face confirmed that clearly enough, so he prepared himself to advance regardless of the dangers.

Melody felt the same churning feeling in her stomach as she had all the other times. The creature at the end of the hallway was slowly moving towards her, defying reality as it pushed the moonlight away from itself as if parting a curtain.
She swung a look over at the clock. 10:23 p.m.

It was time!

She dropped the candlestick holder and raced towards the kitchen, doing her best to avoid looking back. Experience had taught her that would be a mistake.

Mr. Nightmare howled in rage as his intended prey escaped. He slung a thick tentacle into the wall, easily smashing a large hole in it. The moonlight hindered his pursuit somewhat, but his hunger drove him on. He must get to the human this time. He must.

Melody reached the kitchen, and pushing aside a large cabinet, lifted a loose floorboard up, which revealed a small clear vessel. It was yellowed with age and speckled with dirt and cobwebs. A wry smile slid across her face. She knew it would be there, and it was just what she needed.

It was from her childhood, a small remnant from a time long gone. Her mother used to collect bottles from all over the world, filling her house with a wide array of colorful specimens. When Melody began suffering from bad dreams her mother gave her the bottle. She had said it was from Northern Europe, and used to capture moonlight, which was thought to be a purifying aspect of nature. Her mother had instructed her to place the bottle near her window at night when the moon was full and in the morning to hide it where only she knew the location. Simply being aware of its existence would give her the strength and confidence she needed to face her demons. She would be able to defeat anything her dreams could throw at her.

And it worked.

4

Melody used the bottle numerous times to control her nightmares, each time retrieving it from its hiding spot and splashing the captured moonlight into the faces of her tormentors.

But then he came.

She dubbed him Mr. Nightmare and she soon discovered that he, or it, was very adept at avoiding the moonlight. He had infested her dreams continually, each time eventually succumbing to her secret weapon, but only if she made no mistakes. Only if she acted in the same way as the previous times. Any deviations could lead to disaster.

Lifting the bottle up out of its hiding spot proved difficult, but Melody was determined and eventually released it from its dark tomb. Behind her, nearing the kitchen, was Mr. Nightmare in all his deformed glory, grunting and snarling in rage. His fetid breath corrupted the air around him, reeking of running sores and putrefaction.

And then, without warning, he stopped dead in his tracks. He glared with fear at the bright ray of moonlight that was between him and Melody, pondering ways to get through it without too much damage. The other times he had suffered severe injuries; often nearly enough to incapacitate him, but never enough to actually kill him.

Still, he did not want to endure it if he did not have to. With reluctant effort he swatted the light aside as much as he could, and grimacing in pain, started to advance into the kitchen.

Melody thought quickly and ran over to a small window above the sink which had faded black curtains hanging over it. She promptly ripped them down to reveal a large full moon hanging in the clear night sky. Thin beams of pale moonlight flooded in through the glass, settling on the dusty countertop. She then opened the bottle and scooped as much of the light into it as she could before securing the cap back on.

Faint memories of doing the same when she was a child slipped into her mind. Her mother's face appeared in her thoughts as well, reassuring her to use the bottle to defeat her fears.

Mr. Nightmare was almost on her, his slimy bulk shimmying back and forth with agitated excitement. Melody didn't look back but sensed his location. In one swift motion she thrust the bottle high above her head, flicked off the cap and waved it around vigorously.

And then the unthinkable happened. The bottle slipped from her hand and crashed to the floor, sending tiny shards of dirty glass in all directions.

Mr. Nightmare slid up behind her, confident in the fact that she had done something different this time. He relished the freedom he could now exercise.

In a way Melody was actually relieved, her ordeal was finally going to be over. Her mother's face appeared in her mind again, still exhorting the importance of the gift she had given to her daughter.

Melody collapsed to the floor, exhausted and beaten, as a slender tentacle flowed effortlessly around her neck.

ARDEN BLUFF

Sheriff Ted Bonder sighed to himself as he poured a cup of coffee. He knew he didn't need it, but would drink it anyways, in a way a sad testament to his life. Extra caffeine was the next to last thing that he needed.

The caramel brown liquid wafted its aroma into the thick muggy air of his office. The air conditioner had stopped working two days earlier, an unfortunate result of overuse undoubtedly due to the string of ninety-degree days that had settled over Arden Bluff. The machine had sputtered out a few wisps of cool air before wailing its death throes for all to hear.

Normally he would have welcomed such weather. He had grown up in northern Michigan, near Marquette, where anything above forty degrees was seen as something of a heat wave. But for some reason the warm weather in Arden Bluff didn't quite agree with him. It was more suffocating than comfortable.

Sweat trickled down his weathered face and pooled under his chin. When he had took the job two months earlier he had no idea that the conditions would be, for lack of a better word, *crappy*.

Various cracks and pops echoed in the room when he stood up. His spine had a habit of doing that when it corrected itself. A long history of lower back problems had nestled itself securely in his life, an uninvited and unwanted guest who simply refused to leave.

It was just past nine-thirty in the morning in Arden Bluff. The sun was glowing bright in the clear sky, shining its warmth down on the town's empty streets. All in all, it was a picturesque landscape straight out of a John Constable or Gainsborough painting.

He stretched for a moment or two and sauntered over to the front window. Through the dirty glass he surveyed his new town, his new home.

It was like any other small, somewhat isolated city, surrounded by a cropping of steep ridges and narrow valleys, all winding through each other as if in a dream. And for this place it worked. It added a sense of flow to the town, smooth and unrelenting. It was clean. It was charming. It was comfortable, except of course for the stifling heat. But there was something else about it that he couldn't quite put his finger on, something mysterious, possibly even malevolent.

When he had first rolled through town and decided to stay for a while he had no idea that the townsfolk, an interesting group of characters to say the least, would persuade him to not only stay but to accept the job of town sheriff. It seemed that the previous one had dropped dead of a heart attack shortly before he had arrived. And since he was between jobs as it was he felt like he had little choice. And besides, he did have some previous experience in law enforcement.

The streets were quiet, only allowing the warm sunshine and a gentle mountain breeze to disrupt its solitude. The fact that there were no squirrels scampering up trees or birds flying through the air was not lost on him. In fact there weren't any people either. True, it was somewhat early in the morning, but not that early. There should have been some sign of life.

But there was none. The town was an empty shell, void of life or movement. All was quiet.

The sharp ringing of the telephone jarred Ted from his lonely thoughts. He turned towards it, perched on the edge of his desk, and reluctantly reached for it. He felt as if it were mocking him, offering empty promises of help, or at least communication with another person. He knew very well that it hadn't been working for quite some time, nearly a week by his estimation, and the fact that it was now ringing was cause for alarm. He walked over to it and violently yanked the cord from the wall.

But the ringing continued, both in the room and in his head, a contradiction to sanity. He tried to block it out, but without much luck. It was relentless.

"Sheriff? Sheriff Bonder?"

The scruffy, shabbily dressed teenager stood in the doorway. He was holding a sweating bottle of bright red soda pop and sporting a look of such innocence that Ted was suspicious of his intent.

"Can I help you?" He was surprised with himself at how tired he was of saying those words.

The young man hesitated for a moment and then entered the room. He approached the desk and gently set his bottle of soda down on it. Appearing nervous and uncomfortable, he looked around the room, almost as if he expected someone to jump out at him.

"I know you're new in town and all, and I hate to bother ya with stuff already, but I have a problem. One that really needs your attention."

As he spoke his obviously unwashed hair fell down over his eyes a few times.

"Ya see my pa likes his whiskey, so much so that he spends all of his money on it. Buys the stuff by the truckload."

Ted leaned back on his chair. "So your dad's an alcoholic. It's a bad thing but not illegal, as long as he don't drive while drunk that is."

"I know, I know," the boy continued while eyeing the room nervously. "But when he gets drunk he gets real mean." He then proceeded to lift his yellowed t-shirt to reveal a startling collage of bruises that decorated his torso. He looked up for a reaction. "You should see my ma. She usually gets it worse than me."

Hesitancy laced Ted's voice. "Domestic violence. Most authorities tend to look the other way in family matters like that." He waited for a response.

"So you won't do anything about it?" The fear and frustration in his voice was loud and clear. "Nothing at all?"

"Now now, just relax a bit young man. What's your name?"

"Spinder. Josh Spinder, Sir."

9

"Fine Mr. Spinder. I'll look into it." He glanced over at the phone. "I'll see what I can do."

The boy smiled, revealing half rotten teeth. "Thanks sheriff. Here's where I live." He jotted down his address on a scrap of paper and set it down next to his bottle of soda. "Please come over soon sheriff. Me and my ma are real scared."

Sheriff Bonder smiled back at him as he picked up the paper. "I'll be by later today."

Josh walked out without another word. He quickly left the building, leaving behind a strong impact on Ted's conscience, as well as his bottle of soda.

"Hey wait a minute," Ted called out. "You left your..."

But the young man was gone. Ted went to the door and looked down the street, but there was no sign of the boy. Puzzled, he went back to his coffee.

*   *   *   *

Ted felt weak with exhaustion. His throat was restricted with thirst, swollen and dry, and his head ached far beyond any hangover he ever had experienced. The arid heat of Arden Bluff had firmly settled over the town again, suffocating all within its grip. But this heat was worse than any before because it brought with it a warning. It promised something was going to happen, something big and most likely unpleasant. And Ted knew it all too well.

Nearly two days had passed since Josh had visited his office. He felt a connection to the young man, unlike anything he had experienced before, but couldn't explain it. But it was there. Perhaps Josh truly needed help. Maybe Josh was trapped just like he was, searching for any way out he could, but unable to escape, possibly due to his alcoholic father.

A heavy remorse settled over Ted's conscience. He wished he had visited Josh's house. Maybe he would have been able to save him. Maybe.

The phone ringing shattered the silence. It joined forces with the hunger and thirst that had been attacking Ted for the last couple of days, slowly draining his strength and will to live. It wanted him to answer it, to make some sort of connection to the town. Then God only knows what would happen to him. He knew he must do something or he would surely die.

He abruptly stood up from his desk and stumbled over to the door, kicking the discarded phone for good measure. If he simply made a run for it he might just be able to make it, assuming of course that he was able to avoid the townsfolk. Steadying his nerves the best he could he prepared to sprint out into the streets of Arden Bluff. Any fate would be better than simply rotting away in his office, he reasoned with himself. Anything would be preferable to simply waiting for death to come knocking on his front door.

And then he stopped dead in his tracks. Disturbing memories floated into his mind, ones that he was certain he didn't want to experience again. Memories of what had happened when he had left his office to visit Josh's house two days earlier. Memories of what had happened when he had tried to leave his office that same night, attempting to escape under the cloak of night. The things in the town had nearly cornered him, and he had barely managed to make it back to his office. For some reason they couldn't go there, stopping just short of the building. Glaring at him from the street with multi-colored eyes harboring unfathomable hatred and evil.

Fear and self-preservation prevented him from taking another step. Beaten and weary he slumped back into his chair. The clock on the wall ticked away its countdown to his death as he looked around his rubbage-strewn office for the hundredth time. Debris littered every corner. A sarcastic smile slid across his face.

"Haven't had time to clean the place up," he mused to the empty room. "Haven't gotten round to it yet."

The phone was still ringing, only louder than it was before. Its shrill tone pierced his thoughts, thinning his already fragile state of mind.

"Shut the hell up!" he shouted to the inanimate object. "I'm not falling for your damn tricks anymore. Do you hear me?"

Almost as if responding to his words the phone stopped ringing, leaving the room in unsettling silence.

His new job, his new fate, weighed heavily on his shoulders. If only he would have known. If only he wouldn't have stopped in town. If only he would have seen the signs. If only. It seemed his life was full of if onlys, with one sliding into another.

Without a second thought he jumped up out of his chair and went to the front window again. He leaned forward, almost touching the ice -cold glass with his nose. Still no sign of Josh. The streets lay outstretched before him, empty except for the silent warning they issued. He didn't dare step foot outside. He knew what might happen if he did.

"What do you people want from me?" He shouted through the glass. "Why won't you let me leave?"

The people that began to form in the streets of Arden Bluff glared at him with hunger. They were hungry, all of them, and were intent on not letting their prey escape. They rose gradually, but rapidly, from the cracked pavement of the road. Within seconds the streets were littered with hundreds of them.

A hard lump formed in Ted's throat when he began to recognize some the creatures. Mr. Worthy, the cashier at the town market who had told him about his sick mother in Buffalo. Ms. Yasmin, the attractive young teller at the local bank who had offered to help him set up his checking account. And old man Thompson, who ran the local garage.

A smile formed on Sheriff Bonder's face when he recalled the old man camped out on the front porch of the garage. He seemed perfectly harmless then, friendly and polite with a full of head of chalk white hair.

But not now. Now he was deformed, twisted in unnatural and seemingly painful ways. He grinned impossibly wide, yielding an enormous set of jagged fangs. Evil radiated from him, a malicious mockery of a human, cold and distant. He shivered despite the oppressive heat, as the townsfolk looked at him like a pack of wolves surrounding a wounded animal.

Ted searched the group for Josh but didn't see him anywhere. Only fierce, hungry expressions leered back at him. Could the townspeople get to him if he stayed inside his office? Apparently he was safe there, or at least he had been so far. For some reason they stayed away from his office. He retreated away from the window back to his desk.

Outside, the people's increasing numbers were advancing on the building. Scores of the twisted things slithered onward, occasionally bumping into one another, but always moving forward, arms dangling, mouths open.

Ted fell back into his chair, as the cold realization of what was happening, of what the people in the street really were, sapped what little strength he had.

They weren't human. They were all a part of Arden Bluff…literally. The town itself was a living thing, a creature that expanded itself as it fed, engulfing its surroundings, spreading like a cancer. Ted concluded that his office must be a small part that hadn't been consumed yet, perhaps because it was some sort of sacred spot. Or maybe it simply was an area that didn't taste good. But regardless of the reason he was still trapped.

The phone started ringing again, attempting to lure him into answering it. The cord lay on the floor where he had left it, but it still pulsed with energy. It wanted him to answer it, to make a connection to the outside world…or to allow the outside world to make a connection to him. But he wouldn't let that happen, at least not while he had blood flowing through his veins. He stood up and swatted the phone against the wall, where its ringing continued uninterrupted.

And then he noticed Josh staring at him through the front window. His head pulsed with unnatural movement, several large boils oozing a greenish substance, and his elliptical eyes glowed with hatred.

"Sheriff? Sheriff Ted Bonder? I see you." His deformed head titled to one side as if studying Ted. "You were supposed to come out to my house…ya know, to help me and my ma." A new arm sprouted out of his back and flailed high above his head. "You were supposed to come out of there. You should've come to my house."

The sudden realization that Josh was not a young boy who was in need of help stung Ted like a thousand needles. He had believed him. And now the truth was plain to see in all of its deformed glory.

Ted sat down behind his desk, a weary and defeated man. All he had believed in had been shattered right before his very eyes. Everything that had made sense in the world to him, destroyed in a violent and frightening contradiction to sanity. He wasn't sure exactly what his fate would be but he knew it wouldn't be pretty. The things outside his office attested to that fact.

"At least you bastards can't get me in here!" he shouted to the frustrated faces in the windows. "I'd rather rot away from starvation than let you monsters get a hold of me!"

The creatures hissed in anger.

Ted looked at Josh and noticed a slight hint of joy on his sickening features. There was no mistaking it. There, between the festering boils and glowing eyes was a look that concealed a secret. The look froze Ted's spine in place with its promise of victory, of impending domination.

Ted fondled his useless gun and wondered if he ought to use it on himself. Suicide was not a courageous way to go but considering his predicament it seemed like a good way out.

And then he noticed Josh smiling. It was a crooked grin, uneven and twisted, but what really made it unsettling was the direction he was looking in, the side of Ted's desk, or more accurately the wastebasket on the side of the desk. Leaning over Ted peered into the trashcan. There, under various papers and discarded wrappings was the soda bottle that Josh had left that day when he came to Ted for help. Ted had tossed it out when he had cleaned his office up and didn't give it a second thought.

And there was still some red liquid in it.

It churned and bubbled with an otherworldly ferocity. Ted watched in horror as the fluid slid up the sides of the bottle, spilled out of it, and began to crawl up out of the wastebasket.

It moved rapidly, slithering along the floor like a snake, making its way to the front window. The fluid slid up the glass, coating it completely as the creatures howled in excitement.

There was nothing Ted could do but watch as the glass melted away before his very eyes, removing the last barrier between himself and Arden Bluff.

ALL THAT REMAINS

"What was that?" Nick asked while fumbling for the flashlight.

Ryan looked up from his Nintendo DS video game. "Say what?"

Nick finally located the flashlight and quickly flipped it on, spraying the interior of the tent with light.

"I heard something. It sounded kinda like scratching."

"I didn't hear nothing," Ryan retorted while continuing with his game. "You're just being paranoid."

Nick pushed his shoulder length black hair out of his eyes, he had always despised haircuts. Perhaps he was just being paranoid. He still slept with a nightlight on in his bedroom and he couldn't fall asleep without the steady drone of a fan, so maybe his imagination was compensating for the lack of creature comforts that he had become accustomed to.

"Yeah I guess you're right," he admitted to Ryan who was still hypnotized by his video game. "I'm just a little bored that's all."

Ryan let a snicker escape. "Bored? You? You're always doing stuff. You never sit still."

Ryan looked over at his troubled friend. He knew that lately his buddy was having a lot of bad luck. His dad had lost his job, he had caught a case of the flu that was so terrible he had to miss two weeks of school, and then he lost his dog.

"Hey Nick, why don't ya open a book or somethin? You're always reading Stephen King or that Lovecraft weirdo." He instantly noticed that his suggestion was met with enthusiasm. "What's that story about the killer frogs again?"

Nick's eyes light up. "Rainy season. Stephen King wrote it. It's in Nightmares and Dreamscapes."

Ryan laughed out loud, literally shaking the tent. "Yeah, that's the one. That story scared the crap outta me!"

"Yeah me too," Nick replied. His worry about the sounds he'd heard was diminishing. "King did a great job establishing

17

isolation with the setting. And his characters practically felt like relatives!"

Seeing that his friend was in a better mood, Ryan went back to his video game. "Why don't ya read another one and tell me all about it," he offered.

"Sure," Nick said eagerly and reached for his backpack. But after searching through it he realized that he'd forgotten to pack any of his books. The sudden recollection of leaving them in the house popped into his head.

However, another recollection also came to mind, one that was far worse in its implications...the noises he'd heard. Suddenly the prospect of venturing out of the tent, through the backyard and into his dark house to get his books did not appeal to him. But he also didn't dare ask Ryan to go with him. He'd never hear the end of it. He sighed as he realized his only option.

"I'm gonna go to the house and get my books. I forgot them." He could only hope that his fear didn't show on his face.

Ryan only nodded without even looking up from his game. Mustering what little courage he could he grabbed the flashlight and unzipped the tent.

It was a clear, chilly night with a pallid full moon hanging in the sky. Huge oak trees loomed overhead like wooden demons dangling thin arms in every direction as crickets chirped their night songs in the dark. Nick paused briefly and then forced himself to leave the sanctuary of the tent.

The cool night air washed over his face, temporarily refreshing him, but quickly dissipating, leaving him feeling vulnerable and afraid. The house, squatting like an enormous black rock, seemed like it was a miles away. A thin plume of smoke trailed up from the chimney and into the night sky, making it appear to be breathing.

He swung his flashlight over towards his home as if to verify that it wasn't some monster that merely imitated a house.

It wasn't.

18

It was only his familiar home, the same one that he had walked out of a few hours earlier, camping gear in hand. He breathed a huge sigh of relief and began to make his way towards it.

And then he heard to sounds again.

They were the same scratching noises as before, only more pronounced. Part of him wanted to shine the flashlight on them, to reveal what was making them, but part of him didn't want to.

Without thinking he sprayed the ground with light.

He saw only a smooth blanket of damp grass, punctuated by weeds and bare patches. He could still see Ryan's shadow in the tent hunched over the glow from his videogame. It gave him a slight reprieve from the fear that had been plaguing him.

Turning back around, the house now seemed like a safe haven, one that offered protection from the night and all that it contained. He started to walk towards it.

Once inside his home he quickly located three of his favorite books, which he had foolishly left on the kitchen counter, King's 'Nightmares and Dreamscapes', Barker's 'Books of Blood volume three' and his favorite novel, Hodgson's 'The House on the Borderland'. He tossed them into a grocery bag and walked to the doorwall leading to the backyard.

The yard looked ominous, cloaked in darkness and as still as the grave. He could still see the tent however. It looked like a small island floating in a black sea.

Sweat dripped from on his brow and ran down his face. Just why he was so nervous he didn't exactly understand. Was it because he thought he had heard a few noises in his own backyard? It was still the same place he had reluctantly pushed the lawnmower over countless times before. It was still the same place he had learned how to properly swing a baseball bat, a rare case when his neglectful father had found some time to spend with him. It was still the same place where he had watched his beloved dog Bogart run around in before he had succumbed to heartworms.

A tear welled in his eye and cascaded down his cheek when he thought of how Bogart had died. The thought that God would even create those sickening little things made him sick. It seemed their only purpose was to lodge themselves in an innocent dog's heart and snuff the life out of him.

Only a few months had passed since Bogart had died. Nick still clearly remembered seeing his father wrap him up in a blanket and put him into the trunk of the car. He could still hear his parents arguing over the cost of cremation for Bogart and his dad saying that he would take care of it.

His attention swung back to the yard. He would have to cross the sea of darkness to reach the tent, something he didn't look forward to, but staying in the dark house would mean his parents might hear him, which was another prospect he didn't want. With a deep breath he ventured out into the backyard.

He had barely taken five steps when he heard the noises again. They were the same as before, only this time they seemed to be coming from the tent. Ryan's shadow was still visible, hunched over the glow from his videogame. The distance between the house and the tent felt like a mile. Nick wielded his flashlight like a weapon, gripping it so tightly that his hand hurt. The strange sounds clung to his mind like wet cobwebs, each and every one echoing with its mysterious and potentially dangerous implications. He did his best to ignore them, secure in the thought that if he could reach the tent he would be safe.

Eventually he did reach it. He quickly unzipped it and peeled back the fabric, nearly tripping over his own feet to get inside.

"Hey Ryan, I'm back."

His friend didn't even look up.

Nick felt uneasy. Was Ryan feeling okay? Maybe he had too much pop or candy.

"I found my books. Like an idiot I left them in my kitchen."

Still no response. Ryan just sat there with his video game nestled in his lap.

And then Nick felt a cold chill grip his spine. He had noticed something, something small but nevertheless strange.

Ryan was not playing his game. It lay in his lap, on but still. Ryan's hands merely cupped it, but did not play it. It was as if he were in a trance.

"Ryan? What's the matter?"The words felt useless, as if he were talking to a brick wall.

And then he saw it. The movement caught his eye, sending yet another jolt of fear down his spine.

Worms! And not just a few, but dozens…hundreds! They squirmed over each other resembling blind strands of bloody spaghetti vying for sustenance.

Fear and nausea paralyzed Nick where he sat. He tried to scream, to shut himself away from the impossible horrors that were displayed a few feet away from him, but couldn't. He could only stare in disbelief.

Ryan was immobile. The mass of worms he was perched on was thick with movement. They twisted in every direction, and crawled up his arms and chest, leaving sickly trails of bloody slime in their wake. Why he did nothing to shake them off Nick didn't know. Was he hurt? Perhaps paralyzed in some way. Or was he so overcome with fear that his body simply refused to respond?

"Ryan! Let's get outta here! Ryan? Are you all right?"

Ryan looked up slowly and opened his mouth as if to speak and instantly Nick knew what was happening to him. It was at that moment that he realized that just because something is impossible doesn't mean that it can't happen.

Worms spilled out of Ryan's mouth and showered down over his chest. Nick fought the urge to vomit, briefly tasting the remnants of his dinner, but didn't. His fear and disgust kept him from passing out. The worms were inside of Ryan. They were controlling him in some way, manipulating him like some type of twisted marionette.

"Ryan! Ryyaannnn!"

Ryan's eyes closed as he fell over, creating a wet thud as his weight crushed the worms beneath him.

Nick understood now. He knew what the worms were and where they had come from. With courage he didn't realize he possessed he reached forward and gripped the blanket. A sudden jerk with his hand confirmed his fears further.

Bogart's lifeless eyes glared up at him. What was left of his beloved dog lay in a motionless lump, split down the middle like a ripe melon. Inside it was alive with movement, but not with life.

Heartworms! Those sinewy little parasites that had killed his dog were responsible!

The impossibility of the scene was matched only by the horror of it. The worms writhed in violent convulsions, coating the remains of his best friend and his dog with their sickly residue. Nick began to back out of the tent, being careful not to touch anything. Now he knew exactly where his dad had buried Bogart. If only he had put a maker on the grave. If only.

He reached behind himself, feeling blindly for the zipper of the tent. How there were so many of the worms he didn't know. They must have somehow multiplied.

He gripped the zipper tightly and slid it down, exposing the nighttime sky. He quickly glided out of the tent and onto the cool, moist grass of the yard, intent on waking his parents.

But he stopped dead in his tracks when he felt the grass squirming under his feet.

TIME (between fiction and non-fiction)

Professor Vitax rubbed his aching back in a vain attempt to relieve the spasms. They reminded him of a dinner guest who had overstayed his welcome. A slight but chilly breeze floated in from the east raising goose bumps on him, which only added to his discomfort. Fatigue and boredom had joined forces and were battling with his instinct to survive. He wanted to fall asleep but knew very well that that would be a fatal mistake; a glance in the direction of Jonathon's remains reaffirmed that fact.

Jonathon had been one of his brightest students at the university. He had possessed a brilliant mind as well as an incredible imagination, unparalleled by any other person he knew. Professor Vitax smiled to himself as he did his best to ignore the grumbling in his empty stomach.

He had always liked Jonathon and saw great potential in him. He recalled fondly the first time Jonathon had walked into his classroom. He was pencil thin and sported a mismatched set of clothes, the stereotypical nerd. But his intelligence shone through his odd exterior very quickly, overriding any preconceived notions anyone had of him.

He had only been twenty years old but had already managed to successfully fuse his computer-like mind with a seemingly boundless grasp of imagination. He traveled to the outer reaches of possibility and beyond. He would access a situation, weigh all possible solutions and their consequences and apply the most feasible one, regardless of its origins or structure. He was a true genius, undoubtedly capable of great things.

But his life ended far too early and much too violently.

A frown replaced the smile on the professor's face as he again realized his current situation. Jonathon was responsible for it although somewhat indirectly. His advanced mind, coupled with his boundless imagination, had unlocked one of the great and terrifying secrets of mankind. Jonathon had himself remarked that he had resided somewhere between fiction and non-fiction; one of his allegorical labels that he enjoyed placing on himself.

This moniker had allowed him to tap into the realm of fiction while he was researching the aging process and how to best slow it down.

A deep, guttural snarl filtered into the cave from a short distance away. Professor Vitax straightened up and tightened his grip on a tree branch that he had managed to pick up earlier; it was his only defense.

Looking over at the pile of bones that had once been Jonathon invoked an even greater sense of dread in him. He whispered a prayer mixed with a vow of not ending up like his bright student, a promise that he could only hope he could keep.

Jonathon had been nearing a breakthrough and had confided in the professor what he was uncovering. It had been an unusually warm day when he strolled confidently into the professor's classroom. He seemed excited but also agitated and disturbed. The first thing the professor had noticed about him was the sweat, which coated his face and the wild look in his usually placid eyes. He was very close to a breakthrough with his research and needed someone to talk to. The professor set aside the paperwork he was working on and attempted to calm him down. Seeing his brightest student, whom he also regarded as a friend and even a colleague to some degree, stressed to the point of a nervous breakdown was troubling to say the least.

Jonathon was babbling. His words were nearly incoherent and the speed with which he was talking was truly astounding. It was as if his mouth was incapable of keeping up with his brain. The professor strained to decipher them.

Jonathon raved on and on about discovering the true source of time and its origins. He said that time itself was a malevolent entity, possibly even organic in some twisted and incomprehensible way, that was in league with death. The two forever worked together on the demise of everything, from mankind right down to the smallest and most insignificant microbe. Time wielded its most common and effective weapon, aging, the majority of the time but occasionally it struck with a much more devastating form of attack…time displacement. He added that time could not alter reality however but only change when reality occurred. The look in his eyes shocked the professor.

Jonathon took a deep breath and attempted to steady his nerves. After downing a large glass of water he looked the professor straight in the eyes and delivered the most frightening words yet…he was afraid that time was going to come after him.

The professor originally scoffed at his pupil, summing up his erratic behavior to too much work and too little sleep. The possibility that Jonathon could have actually been correct with his results hardly occurred to him; a mistake that he would learn to dearly regret.

A shudder stung his spine as he recalled when he and Jonathon were transported to the place he now found himself in. One minute they were standing in his classroom and the next thing they knew they were running for their lives in a dense predator-filled forest.

He had a completely new perspective on mankind's place in the world. God, time, death, fate, all were powerful forces who controlled all existence. Perhaps they were one in the same; merely different branches on the same tree meting out rewards and punishments at their whim. He could only guess, as anyone would be able to, although his guess would be more educated due to his current situation.

The growl was starting to increase both in its intensity and its tone. It smelled him and knew there was prey nearby.

The professor wondered what fate time had originally planned for him. Maybe it would have been a much less violent end.

It was getting close now. Heavy sniffing and panting punctuated the snarls and groans as it plodded towards the cave where the professor was holed up. A rudimentary excitement filled its pea-sized brain as it swung its thirty- foot long bulk through the foliage.

Professor Vitax lifted the tree branch and held it as tight as his weakened condition would allow. Sweat beaded on his forehead and matted down his thin gray hair to his head; he was ready as he would ever be.

He laughed quietly to himself when he thought about the prospect of calling out for help. It was just the basic reaction of self-preservation, oblivious to the fact that Homo sapiens didn't exist yet, at least not for another one- hundred and fifty million years or so.

The allosaurus poked its formidable snout into the cave opening and sniffed. It sensed prey was near, it could smell it, and although it would be a far smaller meal than the roaming sauropods it was used to devouring, it was much too hungry to pass on it.

Professor Vitax tried to remain still, hoping that the beast would not be able to sense his location. But when the carnivore reared back and crashed its two- ton bulk into the cave, the professor knew he was doomed and braced himself for the fate time had chosen for him.

HUNGER

I must eat. My stomach is twisting and bending in spasms, each stronger than the previous one. I thought I had become somewhat used to the hunger but with each passing minute I realize that I was mistaken. Many hours have passed since my last meal and I am reminded of this constantly. What I must do I do not wish to do but I learned many days ago that it is inevitable…because I must eat. I must attain sustenance or perish, and perish is not an option. My condition is not my fault for I was innocent in my mistake. I was merely a curious passerby with no ill intent in my heart.

The silver bullets in my belly are of little concern to me for their pain pales in comparison to the hunger. An anthill next to a mountain, a puddle beside an ocean, a planet within a galaxy.

I can feel the blood dripping from the wounds coating my body in a sticky layer but I pay it no heed. My sole purpose is to find food. To sustain my life, although I sometimes wonder why I would want to.

I can hear the men in the woods. They're after me, trying to kill me, tracking me down with their guns and torches. I can smell their anger, it is mixed with their fear and it stinks like all hatred does. But I am faster than they are. I know these woods well and my senses are keen. Their searching will be futile.

My thoughts swing back to Louisa, my beautiful and greatly missed wife. The longing that I harbor for her is nearly unbearable. I can still see her smile in my mind, radiating all of the warmth and compassion we shared in our life together. How I wish I could see her again.

I sense movement in the shadows. My eyes, although blurred by my wounds, instantly hone in on the source of the movement.

It is a little girl of no more than five years old. Her long curly locks frame her white face like a painting. She steps out from behind a large tree and looks directly at me, unaffected by my appearance. Her bravery confuses me almost to the point of admiration.

And then I feel her thoughts tap into what is left of my human soul.

"I represent all that you are and all that was done to you."

Is she my salvation? I do not know but I feel compelled to listen to her and not attack.

I open my mouth to reply but only raspy growls escape, which echo through the woods. A werewolf is cursed in many ways. The inability to transfer his thoughts, his human thoughts, to words is but one.

"You need not speak, my poor creature," she says to my mind. "I can sense your needs without the hindrance of words."

Relief washes over me, even temporarily overshadowing the hunger and the pain from my wounds. I relay all of my suffering to her in the hopes that she can somehow ease the agony.

She smiles at me, the first such expression I have witnessed in many moons, and tilts her small head to one side. I instantly feel a wave of relief come over me. She senses the emptiness in my heart for Louisa. She realizes the fear I have for all I come into contact with. She feels the hunger that holds me in its grip. And she knows the anger I have towards the one who was responsible for my condition…the witch who cast this malady upon my body and soul.

She resided near the outskirts of the neighboring hills. I stumbled across her shabby abode while hunting one day. Foolishly, I entered the shack unaware of the power and temperament of its owner.

A lone figure was seated near a small fireplace with a smooth, black cauldron dangling above the flames. She addressed me ominously.

"Fool by thy one who dares to cross my threshold!"

Her words were marred by age but unaffected in their intent. I struggled for a response.

"I…I apologize for the intrusion. Forgive me my ignorance and I shall be on my way." I could only hope that she appreciated my words and the sincerity they held.

But I was wrong.

She pushed something off of her lap and it quickly scuttled into the shadows. I caught a brief glimpse of its hairy body and four pair of eyes looking back at me.
Standing up as much as her arched back would allow she fixed her loathsome gaze upon me. It was a face I shall never forget.

"Filthy traveler from afar," she scowled. "I know not your intent but my wrath shall fall upon you regardless, full in its power and misery." The large mole on her crooked nose twitched grotesquely with each word.

My stomach curled into knots as my lunch threatened to evacuate my body.

"Again, please accept my apologies for the disruption of your rest," I pleaded. "I shall leave you to your peace."

I turned to leave and immediately found myself writhing in the doorway, completely helpless at the feet of the old crone. Even my mouth refused to open.

She stood high above me…too high for any mortal. Her feet hovered at least a foot over my head as she flailed her twisted arms in the air.

"I curse thee to a life of hunger and despair. Oth amaon trunthith ss…"

My head was spinning.

"Nether regions of Thag voorern mossae…"

The words meant nothing to me but I knew their purpose could not be good.

And then my world went black.

The little girl continued smiling at me as if studying the pitiful condition I was in. "I assure you weary traveler that what was done wrong shall be corrected. My promise in this matter is absolute." And then she raised her arms into the air and began to sway from side to side.

I felt the pain from my wounds increase in intensity. My head was growing light and my vision was blurring. Death was seeping into my body and I was powerless to stop it, although I wondered why I would want to. And then I crashed to the ground gasping for breath.

I looked up into the face of the little girl who was standing high above me…too high for any mortal. Something scurried around behind her on many legs, briefly pausing and then moving yet again, as if hiding behind its owner. Her cryptic words accompany me into the darkness.

"You must forgive me, young fool. For I am old and do forget my incantations occasionally. But fear not young fool for I will right the mistake as I had promised you." Her voice thickened with hatred. "Immortality shall be cast down upon you as a suffocating veil of despair. You will never know the release of death."

The small village is within my sight now. A dozen small houses huddle next to each other like children around a fire and I stumble towards them, wary of my surroundings but pushed on by the hunger.

The door is more solid than it looks. Surely there are locks on the other side of it. Nevertheless, I slam into it with all my strength and eventually it gives way. It crashes to the ground, stinging my ears and creating a small dust storm but none of that bothers me for I can smell food. The people who live here are definitely still here…I can sense them.

A stifled whimper from another room catches my ear. I sense movement. There is no door to the room, only a tattered sheet that dangles loosely over the doorway and I easily push it aside and gaze at the occupants.

A thin, pale woman and two small children huddle in the far corner of the room. The moonlight outlines their shapes clearly, showing the fear on their faces. That fear is strong and intensifies when I begin to advance on them.

But then a sharp, burning pain tears into my abdomen. I can feel the blood leaking from the wound as I begin to grow weak and disoriented. I do my best to ignore it but it becomes increasingly difficult to do so. The woman and the children cringe in fear as I crash to the ground in front of them.

Torches enter the room now. They hurt my eyes and singe my body. The men talk excitingly amongst themselves and I can only make out a few of their words in my agony. I hear, "we got him" and "get the woman and children out."

The look on their faces when I rise to my feet is a strong mixture of fear and confusion. I dig out the silver bullets and flick them at the men, all the while growling fiercely and gnashing my teeth. Most of them run away but a few charge at me, torches flailing. My hunger directs my actions as I quickly take them down and begin my grisly feast.

THE DEPTH OF THINGS

Most people don't believe me. They think I'm crazy. But I'm telling the truth. I've seen things that would make you cringe in fear and run back to your mom and dad.

Jerson and Oaks. That's the intersection where I've seen stuff that would make your skin crawl. It's nothing special there, just a spot where two dusty old roads intersect, but there's something else there, something ancient and powerful…and evil.

The first time I went there was just after my big sister had her accident. She was nearly killed when some guy, who shouldn't have even been driving, slammed into her truck. I was curious about where the accident had happened so when she had recovered enough I asked her where it was.

That should've been my first warning that something wasn't right about that spot. She told me that there wasn't really any other car. There was nothing else there. She said it was the ground. And then she told me not to tell anybody else. She was afraid people would think she was crazy.

Her words stuck in my head like glue, but also fueled my curiosity. I had to go to that place. So I enlisted my two best friends, Frankie Unos and Tommy Hadden.

It was a chilly fall evening when we set out for what we were hoping would be a great adventure if nothing else. Boy were we wrong. Frankie was injured real bad and Tommy…well he was killed. The nightmares I get are terrible. I can still see that ground rising up and bursting like a water balloon, spilling out thousands of vicious little bugs. Those things were far worse than any spiders or snakes I've ever seen. We ran for our lives. Tommy though wasn't quick enough.

When Frankie was still in the hospital I visited him. He had a whole bunch of tubes and wires going in and out of him. He looked at me and the fear in his face broke my heart.

"Tommy," he choked.

"I know, I know," I whispered. "He's gone. Tommy's gone."

"No he's not. He's here. He was here last night. I saw him through the window. He was looking right at me."

The words shocked me beyond belief. What did he mean? We both knew that Tommy was dead. We saw him get sucked right into the ground right before our eyes. Was his ghost haunting Frankie now? Or was it that terrible intersection that was manifesting itself in some way to scare us? Either way I was terrified. Normally I wouldn't have believed such stuff but after what I'd seen I didn't doubt it for a minute.

The next day Frankie was dead. He was found in his hospital bed white as a sheet with blood everywhere. I decided that I had to confront my fears and face whatever was at that intersection. So I packed up some food and water and I also took my dad's hunting knife and a baseball bat with me. The next morning I left right after breakfast.

I remember the day well. It was crystal clear outside and unusually warm for that late in the year. I approached the intersection cautiously; fully aware of what had happened the last time I was there. The knife and bat I had gave me a little courage, but not that much. There were no birds overhead, no squirrels scampering around, no crickets chirping. Nothing. Nothing at all but the trees swaying in the wind. Thinking back I would have preferred some noise, anything.

The two roads lay there, crossing over each other like huge dusty snakes. I took a small step into the intersection and then another. I knew something would happen but felt prepared to deal with it. I felt like I owed it to Tommy and Frankie.

When I neared the center of the intersection I noticed that the ground started to ripple like it was made out of water. Then a deep red glow like burning embers began to appear in the dirt. Within seconds it looked like a pool of blood and fire.

This terrible sight had barely registered in my mind when I felt a pulling sensation, similar to a whirlpool. I jumped out of the road as quickly as I could and fell to the ground exhausted. When I looked up a sight beyond any nightmare I could ever imagine cursed my eyes.

Tommy Hadden was rising up from the center of the intersection!

His body was twisted in unnatural ways, limbs bending in opposite directions, his head leaning back so far I thought it would fall off, and the look on his face was a terrible mixture of pain and evil.

I stood up, transfixed by the horrible display in front of me.

"Where do you think you're going?" Tommy roared.

I couldn't answer him. All I wanted to do was run away; even though I knew I wouldn't get too far. He'd find me just like he found Frankie.

"The spot wants you," he moaned. "We want you."

He floated over to where I stood. The realization that I might die then and there settled over me like a cold wet blanket. But I had to be strong. I forced myself to look him in the eyes.

"T...Tommy? Is it really you?"

Tommy's head snapped to one side. A thick crack accompanied the unnatural movement. "Young idiot," he groaned. "What I am is not important. What is important is that you are here now."

I was as confused as I was scared. "What do you mean?" I asked while backing away.

Tommy smiled. "Some places were missed during creation. I am an extension of this spot. The depth of things beneath is infinite. God himself is not perfect. Even he can make mistakes."

As he spoke he floated closer and closer to me.

"There is much more beneath your feet than you realize. Much, much more."

I struggled to speak. My tongue was as paralyzed as my legs. I was a sitting duck. I could only stand and watch my friend...my dead friend, come closer to where I stood. His face dripped bloody slime as oversized serrated teeth mechanically chomped up and down in his mouth.

35

"The barrier is thinning," he hissed. "It will bare all eventually."

I'd seen enough. I knew very well that he was not my friend anymore. I mustered what strength I could and turned tail and ran, not ever looking back.

I don't know how long it took me to get home, but knew it was probably in record time.

$$*\qquad*\qquad*\qquad*$$

The barrier is thinning. The barrier is thinning. It will bare all.

The words puzzled me as much as they scared me. But what did they mean? All I could do is hope I would never find out.

Unfortunately however I did find out, along with everyone else. I think soon every person on the planet will understand the words perfectly. The barrier Tommy was referring to was Earth's crust. It separates us from Hell. And it's thinning; allowing whatever is down there to surface. The deep red glow is under my bed now and as I look out my bedroom window I can see it in the house across the road...Frankie's house. It fills all of the windows there. I'm sure his family is gone by now.

I was raised to believe in God and the Devil, but only in the spiritual sense. I'd never thought of them as being physical beings. But maybe Heaven is a real place, floating high up in the sky. And maybe Hell is also a real place, lurking just beneath our feet, waiting for the protective barrier to thin.

A TENSE SITUATION

Linda watched the doorknob jiggle back and forth as her captive attempted to free herself. But she knew very well that her friend wouldn't be able to escape. She had wedged a heavy chair up under the handle on the door.

"Linda? Answer me dammit!

Marla paused for a moment. "I know you can hear me!"

Linda smiled to herself. "Don't waste your breath Marla. I'm not letting you out. Or at least not yet." She tilted her head to one side as if to emphasize her confidence. "And I think you know why too."

Marla continued to struggle against the door, pushing and hitting it with all of her strength. But it held firm.

"Where's Jason at?" she demanded.

Linda scowled. "You don't need to worry your pretty little head about him." She pushed her long blonde hair back. "He's not your concern anymore."

Marla, straining to control herself, bit her lip in anger.

"Did you kill him too?"

"Listen to me little Miss Innocent," Linda retorted. "You know perfectly well who the killer is here. Don't try to feed me any of your bullshit cause I know better!" A tear welled in her eye when she remembered all that they had been through together. It truly pained her to be forced to lock up Marla but she felt as if she had no choice. "You're probably one of those things. I don't think you're even human! Jason told me he saw your eyes change. He said they were red, blood red!"

Marla fell to the floor of the closet. Exhaustion had taken its toll on her. All she could do was reason with her friend. She could only rely on their friendship and all they had been through to make Linda see reason and let her out.

"Linda, it's me Marla. We've been through so much together. How could you do this to me?" She listened to any signs that Linda was changing her mind. "I'm not any freakin' monster. You know it and I know it. I didn't kill Tommy or Ross or even the damn cat. When I found them they were already dead, all of them."

A long dead silence followed.

"Linda do you hear me? Linda you bitch listen to me! Linda!"

Linda stood up and sauntered over to the bed. Lying down, she kicked off her pink tennis shoes and stretched herself out.

"Jason will be here any minute ya know," she teased. "He told me we were gonna find out if you're human or not." She sat up in the bed and pushed her long blonde hair back over her shoulders. Her eyes tightened into a squint. "Oh and he's bringing Tommy and Ross with him too."

Marla stood up and rubbing her swollen eyes concentrated on the door. Thin plumes of wispy smoke floated up from her head, filling the closet with its thick aroma. With one swift wave of her hand the closet door crashed to the ground as if made of cardboard.

"I do hope those bastards hurry up," she grunted in a deep, guttural tone. "I'm starving. I haven't eaten in months."

At that very instant Jason, Tommy and Ross burst into the room.

"Hello ladies, we're here!" they all laughed.

Tommy and Ross fell onto the bed, flanking Linda who was smiling from ear to ear. "What took you guys so long?" she asked. "We've been waiting forever."

Tommy snapped his hands back releasing two-inch long talons from their sheath. "You know we had to wait till the right time baby. We couldn't show up earlier."

Ross was swinging his arms around his head as if he were doing some sort of bizarre ritual dance, his face a mixture of pleasure and pain. In a split second one of his hands swung near Linda's head, slicing off one of her ears, which landed across the room in a thick bloody pile. Linda only laughed.

"Is he here yet?" Jason asked. "I'm getting hungry." His eyes had become such a deep shade of red they were nearly black.

"You moron," Marla spat. "Of course he's here. Who do you think is narrating this horror story?"

"Could be a girl," Linda giggled. The side of her head where her ear had been was thick with blood. It contrasted strongly with her smile. "They taste good too."

Marla nodded. "I stand corrected. He, or she, fell into our trap perfectly." Her elongated fingers clenched in excitement. "And as usual they don't have a clue."

And then the entire group, Linda, Marla, Tommy, Ross and Jason, all turned and looked at me. Their hungry, red eyes glowed with an evil hunger beyond description, content in the knowledge that I was doomed.

I had been foolish enough to fall for their ploy, to involve myself in their situation, to care about what happened to their characters. And now I was trapped.

I can only watch helplessly as they advance towards me with grins too wide and teeth too long for any human. Hopefully they won't see you as well.

A PART OF CARS FOREVER

The small-block Chevy gyrated slightly to each side as it idled at eleven hundred rpm. Each piston was in perfect harmony with its neighbor and together they created a smooth rumble which exuded power from every cubic inch.

Bryan had fallen in love with that sound as any nineteen-year-old car enthusiast would have and he discovered that he needed a daily dose of it, much like people with their morning cup of coffee. He wanted to be a part of cars forever.

Growing up around his father's garage shop had taught him many valuable things over the years. He had learned as much about running the business as he had about cars and his childhood was full of fond memories, virtually all of which related to cars.

The motor abruptly stopped when Bryan turned the key off. The temperature gauge, one of several mounted above and below the dashboard, was inching its way towards the two hundred and sixty degree line. He feared that the radiator was unable to cope with the increased compression he had incurred when he had the heads shaved. A ten and a half to one ratio would need additional cooling methods, that much was becoming painfully obvious.

Clouds resembling dirty cotton balls silently began to hover overhead. Their belly's swelled with rain droplets and a brisk wind started to bend the trees along the street.

Bryan had hoped to change the rear axle oil and install his new rear end chrome cover but that seemed unlikely now. He shook his head in disgust and continued checking the various reservoirs in the engine compartment.

His attention was suddenly diverted to the reflection gazing down at him in the chrome valve cover.

"Morning," the reflection said politely.

Bryan quickly inserted the power steering cap back on the container and straightened up. "Good morning," he replied uneasily.

"Name's Rick." He reached out a thin, almost delicate hand. Bryan shook it but let go quickly.

"Just moved in down the street. Saw your ride in the driveway so I figured I'd come on over."

"Bryan. Bryan Santo." He never cared for meeting new people but at least he was on his home turf.

"That a three twenty-seven?" The man's large nose twitched slightly making his peach fuzz mustache raise and lower. He reminded Bryan of a mouse, small and always active.

"No, it's a three- fifty." Bryan turned to get his socket set.

The man shook his head in agreement. "Three-fifty huh? Good solid motor. I prefer a big block myself. My Corvette has a three ninety-six. Tunnel ram duals too."

Bryan stopped in his tracks. Dual quads? Maybe this guy wasn't so bad after all.

"Holly six hundreds," he said while bending down to check Bryan's custom wiring job. "She's turned high tens at the track. Thinking about nitrous too. I try to add something new every month or so." He was leaning so far into the engine compartment he could have touched the oil pan. "Put a roll cage in back in March although I haven't been able to use it yet, thank God." Both men laughed.

Rick tugged his blue jeans up only to have them slip back down an inch or two after which he would pull them back up again. His thin physique caused his clothes to dangle on his body like a flag on a pole.

"Have you had her dyno'd yet?" Bryan asked while thinking that Rick's entire wardrobe probably consisted of jeans and t-shirts.

"Yeah, four-hundred and ninety horses, course that's before I added the second carb."

Bryan gulped hard. He had to see this car.

The garage door lifted smoothly to reveal a snow-white sheet contoured exactly to the shape of a classic Corvette.

"I call it the Beast," Rick said through a smile, a smile almost as wide as Bryan's. "She drinks one-hundred and two octane but she's completely street legal...and very reliable too."

Bryan waited anxiously for the cover to come off. He always liked Novas and this one sounded like a beauty. His eyes fastened on the bump in the middle of the hood, a telltale sign of a tunnel ram setup.

Rick pulled the cover off in one swift motion, exposing the cherry red Nova Super Sport underneath. Bryan's eyes nearly popped out of his head. It was perfect.

"I haven't taken her out on the road in a while but I'm getting ready to, kinda thinking about putting on nitrous first." He motioned to a brand new set of boxes stacked on a nearby workbench. NOS was stamped boldly on each one.

He quietly walked to the driver's side door, opened it and smoothly sat down in the seat.

The garage shook when the engine came to life. The twin carburetors shifted every time the motor revved. And then Bryan heard the words he had been waiting for.

"Wanna go for a ride?"

Heads from all directions turned when the Nova thundered by. Bryan felt like the coolest guy in town, being seen in such a car. His heart skipped a beat when Rick asked if he wanted him to "get up on it a little."

His neck nearly snapped when Rick punched the pedal to the floor. He wasn't sure but he could swear he only saw sky through the windshield.

But then just as suddenly Rick eased up on the pedal. The car immediately slowed as the engine subsided to a sporadic idle.

"What's the matter?" Bryan asked, seeing obvious frustration on Rick's face.

"She's hungry again," he mumbled to the dashboard. His hands were nervously tapping the steering wheel like a teenager on his first car date. A lump formed in Bryan's throat.

"Eats parts huh?" he asked uneasily.

"You can say that again. Seems like every time I push it she wants more."

"Wants more?"

Rick gave him a somber look. "I'm sorry. I really liked you. You seemed like a cool guy."

Bryan's stomach turned. He felt like screaming but he found it was impossible to open his mouth. In fact, it was impossible to move at all.

"She'll hold you in her gas tank till she needs you...probably a day or two."

Bryan began to feel a burning sensation radiate from the seat. It grew in intensity to such an incredible level that the Devil himself would have backed away from it. Inch by painful inch it enveloped his body until finally he passed out.

He awoke to find himself surrounded by a cold, acidic liquid. He could not smell it but there was little doubt in his mind what it was...gasoline, one hundred and two octane gasoline. Struggling to maintain his sanity proved to be the most difficult thing he had ever done and what awaited him attacked his imagination unceasingly.

The rumble of the engine jarred him back to reality. It seemed miles away and yet close enough to hear clearly. Bryan fought with all his might to resist the suction that was attempting to pull him out of wherever he was but it was too strong. Before long he was being shot through a small tube at an incredible speed. The pain was excruciating, almost unbearable, and if he could have killed himself just to make it end he would have.

He was now imprisoned in some type of small container. Its confines were much more compact than the other container he was in and he began to hear voices.

"Been dyno'd at four hundred and ninety horses, course that's before I added the second carb."

It was Rick!

"I call it the Beast. She drinks one hundred and two octane but she's completely street legal...and very reliable too."

44

An adolescent sounding voice mumbled something like "cool."

"Just added nitrous too," Rick added with pride. "Thinking about putting in a bigger cam. I try to add something new every month or so."

Bryan felt the various bumps and turns as the car rolled down the street. He heard Rick talking with his passenger, telling him more information about the car. Both men laughed and Bryan could hear the excitement in the young man's voice. Then he heard Rick mention something about nitrous.

"Alright, hold on," Rick chuckled loudly.

Bryan was jettisoned forward through a small tube and down into the internal workings of the engine. He would have screamed but he was incinerated in the combustion chamber in a fraction of a second. He had gotten his wish after all…he was a part of cars forever.

APPEARANCES

Larry yawned lazily as morning fatigue hindered his movements. He paid it little attention however as he ran his clammy palm across his cheek and sighed drearily as it met with three days worth of stubble. This too, he decided could wait, promising himself between yawns that he would shave that evening.

"Morning Buddy." The shaggy mix breed hardly moved. Larry could only tell the dog heard his greeting by the small tufts of hair above each of its eyes that shifted slightly as the dog's eyelids raised. "Can see your as awake and alert as I am this morning." Again, barely a response.

He began humming the new tune he'd been working on. A catchy number in E and F Minor. Just needed a smoother bridge. Maybe he'd force feed it to the guys at the next practice. His eyes caught a glimpse of the dusty owl clock dangling silently above the overworked microwave. It displayed seven twenty-five boldly as if taunting him about being late for work. He grabbed his jeans and sprinted towards the messy bathroom. Mr. Cupple would have his ass in a sling if he was late one more time.

Seven- thirty came much too quickly as did seven thirty-five. Seven- forty finally saw him heading towards the door. Buddy took little interest in his owner as Larry shouted "see ya later Bud." The dog rotated to its right side slowly and promptly drifted back to sleep.

Larry did notice something else as he was moving towards the door...a reflection in the microwave glass...leering at him. A malevolent face full of hatred and evil stupidity. Several mutated eyes blinked in grotesque unison, each a foul mirror to a dark and obscene soul.

"Morning butthead," Larry quipped to the monstrosity. He had begun to think that it wasn't going to show up this morning as it had so many other mornings."Hate to see you too."

47

He tapped on the glass and the thing scowled as if trying to destroy its tormentor with its violent expressions.

Seven forty-two and the kitchen door slammed shut, knocking down a bless this mess sign that hung nearby.

The morning D.J. on WZAP babbled on and on about an overpaid celebrity who'd recently parked his Porsche in someone's front room. And to make matters worse, his cheap radio barely got any other stations in, so he was forced to listen.

"Johhny Topaz of *People and Money* fame claims his foot simply slipped off the brake causing his 911 to careen …blah, blah, blah."

He clicked the radio off.

Up ahead, the light switched from green to yellow followed immediately by red. Directly underneath the light, as if dangling by an invisible chain, were three disembodied heads. Each bore a faint resemblance to the aliens in a recent horror flick Larry had rented, although these were unquestionably uglier. All three glared down at him as his Toyota gradually came to a stop. Bloody droplets drifted down in a sickening sprinkle onto the hood of the car.

"Do you guys mind?" he yelled out the side window. "I don't have time to hit a car wash this morning." He then realized that a man and woman were staring at him from their neighboring car. Feeling foolish, he quickly rolled up his window and looked straight ahead, hoping to minimize his embarrassment.

Sometimes he would forget he was the only one who could see the "appearances" as he dubbed them. Been that way since he was a kid, especially the first time. He was nine, maybe ten, in the grocery store with his mom. His mind was alternating between the homerun he'd hit the day before and Susan Bannert. Then the face appeared. A noxious, corrupt face. A face which oozed foul excretions from every orifice. A face which situated itself between Crispy Cups and Corn Flakes. A face whose bloody eyes bore through Larry like a drill through Styrofoam.

His mind initially rejected it as a hallucination. A hideous and unwholesome result of late-night Hershey bars or too many horror movies. But the face didn't vanish as hallucinations do when one's eyes are blinked and the mind cleared. Instead it tilted its deformed head to one side as if pondering how to get at its observer.

Several hours later, Larry found himself wedged tightly underneath his bed. His Mom had chased him around the store with him screaming at the top of his lungs. Fatigue reflected on her face as she pleaded with him to tell her what was wrong.

The memories choked his mind. He remembered how it took nearly two days for him to leave the sanctuary of his bedroom.

Dr. Thantan helped little, due to the fact that he simply could not stop the visions from coming. He merely helped Larry understand why he reacted the way he did but not how to accept it, probably due to the fact that he did not believe Larry any more than anyone else.

Almost three months had passed before he witnessed his next appearance. An enormous entity, roughly twenty feet high, which clung precariously to the side of the Metro Building near downtown. Glistening with slime, its nauseating form seemed to be headless, a great unfinished painting of horror. But Larry noticed it did have a head, one which writhed as its appendages did. Two clouded orbs gyrated rapidly in all directions before eventually focusing directly on Larry. His dinner turned in his stomach like a blender. He sank back in his seat, trying to put as much distance as possible between it and him.

Why had no one else seen it? Why was he being singled out?

Because they're not real. It's just your overactive imagination.

Yes, imagination.

He eventually accepted this, although partly because the other option was much less pleasant.

Time eventually allowed him to ignore the appearances somewhat almost as one would instinctively look away from a burn victim or an excessively obese person. That's not to say that there weren't times when they would bother or even startle him, but overall he learned to handle it well. Life's responsibilities took center stage and diluted the episodes substantially. When a ….thing…. would show itself, Larry would just shrug it off and concentrate on what he was doing.

The Toyota hummed along the road as he began to feel at ease with the upcoming work day. He noticed a large clock in front of Kant Bank. It displayed the time with a heartless reality. Eight twenty-two. Hardly enough time to cover the distance between him and Mr. Cupple's annoyed stare. His foot depressed the gas pedal.

He gave the octapod creature, which was splayed out near a mailbox, little notice. "Don't have time for your ugly butt," he mumbled to the car's interior, feeling a small sense of satisfaction.

Once at work, he decided to try and be as quiet as possible. He was four minutes late and he didn't feel like hearing Mr. Cupple's rhetoric about punctuality.

"Did you kick up the heat?" asked Josie. Her baby blue eyes were framed perfectly by her strawberry blonde hair. Larry stammered for a reply which wouldn't make him sound too stupid.

"Umm..yeah, it's hot in here." Not exactly smooth but sufficient.

"I turned the heat up," announced Mr. Beath. "Better for my allergies. Aren't you a little behind this morning, Larry?" His left eyebrow raised slightly.

"I'm just getting my morning cup of coffee, sir." A small delay in the response raised Larry's hopes that the big boss man wouldn't be sore at him for being late, but it was not to be.

"Well, make it snappy. I don't pay you to get drinks…or be late."

Larry exhaled heavily as Mr. Beath sauntered down the hallway. So much for a quiet morning.

Looking over the day's truck schedules, he mentally mapped out the day's work. Lunch came quickly, largely due to the workload, and two o'clock was not far behind. The day was moving along smoothly for Larry and his mind was gradually shifting towards dinner, a beer and more beer.

Three twenty-five was the time when Emery, Mr. Cupple's scrawny assistant, made his unwelcome showing at the door. "Larry, got that new equipment straightened out yet?" His coke-bottle glasses raised and lowered with the movement of his tiny mouth. Larry felt like throwing a wrench at him.

"On it right away, Emery." He thought the twerp looked kind of stupid, standing in the doorway glaring at him, completely unaware of the arachnid-type thing that dangled a mere three feet above his oversized head. It sent down a slimy tendril which grazed Emery's shoulder.

"Good. Mr. Cupple wants to see you at four sharp in his office. Something about backorders from last week." And with a quick one-eighty, he was gone. Larry slumped into a nearby chair.

"Sometimes I wish I could control you assholes," he mumbled to the dangling creature. It merely cocked its head to one side and hissed.

Mr. Cupple's office door loomed ahead, daring Larry to open it. God, how he hated that office. Reluctantly, he placed three timid knocks on the large, oak door. No reply. Again he knocked, this time with slightly more force. Still no answer. A glance at his wristwatch confirmed the time, three fifty-eight. Well, he was early. If anyone could appreciate that it would be Mr. Cupple. But why wasn't he in his office?

Mrs. Teamont sat placidly at her desk with her usual blank look, tapping away at her computer. She was oblivious to his presence.

"Is Mr. Cupple in?"

She hesitated from her tapping only long enough to answer in a robotic tone.

"Mr. Cupple wasn't feeling well after lunch and asked not to be disturbed." She then resumed her secretarial duties.

51

"But he wanted to see me at four o'clock," Larry retorted, irritated by the prudish redhead's attitude.

"Not to be disturbed," she replied without a glance.

Fine. So much the better. Now he wouldn't have to meet with him. He'd worry about it tomorrow. He strolled back to the docking bay thinking about five o'clock.

The ride home was blissfully uneventful, completely void of traffic or, more importantly, appearances. Buddy was sprawled out not more than six inches from where he had been that morning. He lifted his shaggy head, acknowledged Larry's return and promptly dozed back off. Got to get a younger dog.

The remote control felt good in his hand but the stock market wasn't kind, it showed a two hundred and six point drop for the day. A lame eighties sitcom, which used to be funny fifteen years earlier, clogged another channel.

He finally settled on channel eleven news. Gwen Winsett's beautiful face stared back at him. She was his favorite newscaster. He hardly noticed that the volume was practically off. As he pressed the button to increase the level he nearly choked as Severen Industries came on the screen. Yellow crime scene tape swung in the wind across the front door, the same front door he had passed through only an hour earlier. Numerous police cars were scattered around the front entrance as officers were taking notes and talking with people, including Mrs. Teamont who was showing some emotion for the first time.

"A Mr. Henry Cupple was found murdered in his office earlier today. His secretary, Theresa Teamont, discovered the body and immediately phoned the police. Apparently, he had been decapitated.

Sergeant Milanski of Beachwood Police said it appeared his head had been bitten clean off. No trace of it has been found nor were there any signs of forced entry. Mrs. Teamont..."

Larry clicked the television off. He stared at the blank screen. The thought that Mr. Cupple could have been in that condition when he was knocking on the door made him feel like throwing up. Could that door have been the only thing separating him from a similar fate? He felt a cold shiver run down his spine.

Then the phone shattered the silence.

"Hello?"

A cool, raspy voice was on the other end. "Mr. O'Hara?"

"Yes."

"This is Detective Alad from Beachwood Police. I'd like you to head down to the station if you would for a few questions. There's been a murder at your place of employment and I understand you were one of the last ones to see the victim... a Mr. Cupple ."

"He wanted to see me in his office but I was told he wasn't feeling well," Larry replied nervously. But then he realized he had nothing to hide, he didn't kill him. "I'll be there in a half an hour."

"Thank you Mr. O'Hara and the line went dead.

With a sandwich in his hand, he headed for the door. Out of habit, he glanced at the microwave. Butthead was not there. "Good," he said to himself. "Not in the mood for that shit anyways."

The doorknob was in his hand when the thing in the microwave reflection viciously tore out his throat. And at that same moment all over the world, evil, corrupt things made their appearances before they attacked.

STEPPING STONES

Her mother's eyes.

Those beautiful baby-blue windows to her mother's gentle soul. They were one of the things about her mother that she had loved the most. No matter what kind of trouble she was in she could always depend on those soft, loving eyes to convey the fact that she wasn't really in too much of a dilemma.

Taryn tried her best to relax as the memory played itself out in her mind as it had done so many times before. In it, she was only a young child, perhaps six or seven years old, standing on trial in the kitchen. Warm beams of sunshine filled the tiny, quaint room, illuminating every dust particle in it. Her mother stood before her, judge and jury rolled into one. The evidence of her crime, shards of brightly colored glass, lay across the floor in a neighboring room, plain for all to see. They were all that remained of her mother's beautiful dish set.

She had known perfectly well not to play near the collection, which her mother had prized above all her other worldly possessions. Her mother had made it crystal clear to her on many occasions not to ever touch the dishes, or even go near them, for she had spent a sizeable amount of time collecting them and reveled in showing them to anyone who entered the house.

Outside, a clear breezy day in 1960s Indiana beckoned to her with its promise of play, making the requirement of the disciplinary actions she was receiving all the more difficult to endure.

Taryn recalled what had happened on that long gone summer morning very clearly. The memory had been the same every single time she relived it.

But not this time. This time there were a few things different in it. Her mother's eyes had changed slightly. The warm, baby-blues were gone, only to be replaced with a color unlike anything she had ever seen before. In fact, she could hardly place them in any category of colors she could think of. The best label she could affix to them would be a mixture of dirty yellow and something akin to burnt orange, only darker. This color was undeniably malevolent, and the change altered her beloved mother's visage into a weird mockery of something not even remotely human. The new eyes were clearly hiding something dark, possibly even dangerous.

Her mother's actions had changed as well. The gentle slap she had received on her wrist for her misdeed had become harsher, eventually even drawing blood.

Taryn knew perfectly well that isn't what had happened on that clear Indiana day all those years ago in her mother's kitchen, but it was how she remembered it.

And then came the memory that truly had her doubting her own sanity.

It was a more recent one, perhaps ten or twelve years earlier. In it her best friend Josie, who was practically like a little sister to her, was introducing her to the newest craze in music…disco.

"It's sooo cool," Josie wailed as her head swung back and forth to the monotonous beat. "You can really dance to it."

Taryn smiled to herself as she recalled Josie's long, auburn hair flailing around her swinging head that warm afternoon in her old bedroom.

"It's sooo cool. You…can …really…kill…to…it." Josie's dirty yellow eyes looked into Taryn's. "The Bee Gees are so cute, and they can really sing too." The burnt orange glow in her eyes was beginning to overshadow the yellow, contrasting with her beautiful complexion.

A chill that swept down Taryn's spine snapped her back to the present. Josie had never said that. She was one of the sweetest, most fun-loving people she had ever known. She never would have said anything like that. And the eyes. They were the same unnatural shade as her mother's were.

Again, Taryn knew very well that's not what had really happened in her bedroom with Josie, but it was how she remembered it. And there were other memories also, some as recent as a week ago. They were usually irrelevant, meaningless recollections that would periodically pop into her head, but they were vivid nonetheless.

There was the one when she opened her mailbox and discovered a birthday card sent to her house by mistake. Her neighbor, old lady Marmoun, was in her front yard trimming her hedges at the time. She glanced over at Taryn and waved, as an oily smile slid across her face. Her yellow-orange eyes meshed with her loud muumuu perfectly.

"Oh, hi dear," Taryn recalled her saying. "Just cutting, cutting, cutting. Have to keep the shrubs in order you know." She swung the hedger up over her straggly hair, the blades gleaming in the sunshine. "Have to cut…cut…cut. All the time…CUT…CUT…CUT!"

That was not what had happened, Taryn was certain of that, but it was what she remembered. She recalled what the weather was like that day, sunny with a hint of humidity in the air. She recalled what time of the day it was, approximately nine in the morning. And she recalled that Mrs. Marmoun's eyes were normal. She knew they were.

But the event in her mind said differently.

Was someone, or something, altering her memories? But how, and more importantly why? She had always treasured those images of times gone, frequently turning to them for comfort, and the thought that someone could actually invade the only true sanctuary anyone really had, their mind, disturbed her greatly.

Later that night she was preparing for bed when another random memory floated into her mind. This particular one was cause for great alarm for two reasons.

One: that the handsome young newscaster on her television screen was glaring at her with dirty yellow eyes that were tinged with a burnt-orange glow.

And two: that she had just shut off her television right before walking into her bathroom. It couldn't have been more than five minutes earlier.

She spit out the toothpaste in her mouth and ran to the TV Switching it back on she frantically waited for the handsome young newscaster to come on the screen. When the weather section of the news was over the camera swung back to the two anchors. Much to her relief the young man's eyes were perfectly normal.

Was she losing her mind? Maybe, but the stubborn part of her personality refused to accept it. Her mother had always instilled in her the importance of believing in yourself. No doubt her mom would have felt bad for her if she were still alive. The thought that her only daughter was crazy probably would have killed her sooner than the cancer had.

She switched the television set off and walked over to her bed. The prospect of seeing a psychiatrist weighed heavily on her mind, but she couldn't deny it to herself that it might be the right thing to do.

The room was bathed in darkness when she flicked the lamp off. Shadows hung in every corner of the room, threatening with their power over her imagination, wielding it like a weapon. Outside of the small window opposite her bed a pale full moon dangled in the clear nighttime sky. It glared at her like a wolf gazing at a herd of sheep. She contemplated shutting the blinds but found herself dozing off already, content in the fact that what she really needed was a good night sleep.

And then a sudden and unnerving thought interrupted her rest. She sat up in bed with a cold sweat on her body. Her nightgown stuck to her flesh, further increasing the discomfort and her head spun, wracked by the implications of her revelation. How she had not thought of it before she didn't know, it was so obvious.

Each memory she had where certain aspects became distorted somewhat was more recent than the one before it. The memory in her mother's kitchen with the broken dishes was as far back as she could recall. The most recent one was the television newscast man, which was just a short while ago. Someone or something was using her memories as stepping stones to reach the present…to reach her.

The eyes, a sickly combination of dirty yellow and burnt orange, glared at Taryn from the closet. Slowly, painfully, the thing emerged from its dark hiding spot, all the while keeping an eager gaze on the young woman panicking on the bed. It had been a long and difficult journey for it and it desperately needed nourishment.

With lightening speed and deadly accuracy it fell upon its prey.

AN OLD NEGLECTED CEMETARY

The gash on his palm was beginning to throb. A small crimson lake was forming, speckled with tiny grains of dirt which stuck to the cut like glue. The possibility of infection crossed his mind but he pushed it aside. He had to focus on the task at hand...getting into the cemetery.

Several obscene words directed at the rusty padlock and the unseen wires around it escaped his lips and drifted up into the swaying, leafless October trees. He knew the gate would not open but he still grasped the lock anyways and paid a painful price for it. But it would be worth it, he reasoned to himself. To finally get some answers about the old place would be worth the price of admission.

The cemetery had always been a source of morbid fascination for him. He'd passed it countless times dating as far back as he could remember. He recalled riding his bike, newspaper bags dangling in the back, past the old graveyard on his way to his route every day of the week. Even then, the wrought iron fence which encircled the grounds was intimidating. Back then it had seemed twenty feet high, an untouchable barrier which mocked those who wished to pass through it.

Why they kept it locked in the first place always puzzled him. His dad had told him it was to keep vandals out. He said punks would desecrate the graves and tear up the ground, even though there was more weeds and dirt than grass.

Indeed the graveyard was an enigma. A three-quarter acre silent companion which peered at him as he peddled his rusty yellow bike and newspapers past it every day.

Sometimes he even caught himself looking back at the museum of death half expecting to see desiccated hands clawing their way through the soil which had served as a prison for them for so long. Mindless things that life had passed by whose only link to the memories of man was a stone or wooden ledger with their lives condensed into a name and birth and death dates.

He felt embarrassed every time he turned his head. He, Paul Samath, a young man who had a great deal of common sense falling victim to frightening and alluring but nonetheless impossible scenarios. He knew better. He always prided himself on his firm grip on reality, even when that reality was attacked by old graveyards full of weathered and tilted tombstones.

The pain in his hand jolted him back to the present. The wrought iron fence loomed in front of him, circling the grounds as a mother would a child. It had lost most of its paint to time but still exuded a powerful aura. He took a deep breath and vaulted himself as high as he could. He clenched the horizontal bar along the top of the fence and jammed his feet against two of the brick pillars that were stationed evenly apart. With an effort that pleasantly surprised him, he easily lifted himself up to and then over the top, carefully avoiding the studded spikes along the edge.

His hand was bleeding worse now, leaving its bloody trail behind him. Ripping a small piece of his shirt along the bottom, he wrapped it tightly around his palm. He hated to lose his shirt, he had received it as a birthday gift, but his need for a tourniquet was greater.

Surveying his surroundings he took in the morbid yet interesting sights. His curiosity had gotten him into this situation and now it needed to be quenched completely.

Dozens and dozens of grave markers greeted his eyes. Ancient, neglected things that were intermittingly scattered throughout the grounds. Many tilted severely as if they were in the process of falling over. He looked over the crumbling memorials whose epitaphs were barely legible and whose sole purpose was jeopardized by time and the elements. Most were similar in size and shape, ranging from small wooden crosses to granite slabs, but a few were large obelisks well over six feet tall.

He gathered up all the common sense he had accumulated over the course of his life. He wielded it like a weapon to stave off the irrational fears that such a place would undoubtedly spawn. There were no zombies pulling themselves free from their graves. There were no ghosts malevolently floating between the headstones. There was no evil, unseen force emanating from the ground. There was nothing but an old, neglected cemetery with a somewhat foolish twenty-two year old man standing alone near its center. A young man whose whole existence had been spent rationalizing every aspect of his life, always seeking to logically explain every anomaly and to understand everything beyond his comprehension.

And yet this same young man finds himself alone in a cemetery, inexplicitly drawn to it. A pupil anxious to find out the answers from his mute teacher.

The blood began to soak through the makeshift bandage as he tried his best to ignore it. He had to find out the reason he had come here. He had to understand what was happening to him.

He began to frantically search the grounds, hoping for a clue or a sign of some sort. He scanned the stone ledgers all around him, not knowing what he was looking for or where to find it. The reminders of mortality seemed to look back at him; silent stone and wooden faces reluctant to reveal their secrets. The inscriptions on most were too weathered to read but he managed to make out a few lines on several.

A.H. Jonesh   born July 3, 1915   died Aug. 7, 1937
Mariah Nettle   born Nov. 14, 1923   died Dec. 3, 1945
Benjamin Tether born March 23, 1900 died July 22, 1922

Names that were meaningless to him. Names and dates that offered no insight to the ever-increasing desire he felt for answers. He fell to the ground and cupped his face in his hands, ready to accept defeat.

Then one marker caught his eye. A small cross, darkened with age, not more than two feet high, sitting quietly off to his left amid a row of much larger headstones. Why he noticed it he wasn't sure at first but it became clearer as he moved closer to it. The inscription literally knocked him down.

*Paul Samath beloved son born July 3, 1982 died Oct.
17, 2004*

October seventeenth two thousand four, that was today!
He felt his head grow light as he struggled to keep standing. The
chances of someone with the same name being buried in this
cemetery were a million to one. And what about the dates? July
third was his birthday. Did this mean he was destined to die
today? His whole life was spent seeking logical and sensible
explanations but now he was standing four feet from an
unexplainable and disturbing fact. A fact in the form of a small
cross in an old neglected cemetery.

The throbbing in his hand was steadily increasing.
Looking down, he saw that a small pool of blood was forming.
Before his eyes, the blood rapidly soaked into the ground. As
more drops hit the dirt they would vanish immediately. He turned
his head and looked behind him at the path he had come earlier.
The trail of blood was completely gone. Not a single drop
remained, not even on the fence he had climbed to get into the
cemetery.

Clearing his head proved to be difficult. There had to be
an explanation. There must be a logical, reasonable explanation.

When he suddenly realized what was really happening,
the sheer absurdity of the explanation almost caused him to
hesitate. Fortunately for him he did not for he barely managed to
escape the cemetery before it rumbled to life in an ear-splitting
shriek of inhuman noise.

Safely outside the confines of the fence, he looked on in
horror as his twisted, disturbed and all too real thoughts
manifested into reality before his eyes. The cemetery thing lifted
its tombstones, or rather its bait, high into the chilly October air
before crashing back down again in a malevolent chorus of evil.
He could see it writhing just beneath the fallen leaves and twigs,
full of rage that its prey had escaped.

He peddled as fast as he could trying to escape what could
not possibly be.

After he rode a hundred or so feet he gave in to the curiosity that had outlined his life and turned his head back in the direction he had so quickly left moments earlier. The cemetery was still there, as silent and intriguing as it had always been.

IMAGINATION

The shadow danced off the far wall. Its movements were natural, like a tree branch swaying in the wind, but still unsettling nonetheless. And unlike a branch in the wind these movements suggested life.

Ricky rubbed his sore eyes, as much to confirm that what he was seeing was real as to clear his head. Beads of cold sweat trickled down his forehead and into his eyes. The slight stinging sensation bothered him a little, but not enough to take his eyes off of the shadow. It was a strange thing that demanded his attention.

"W…who's there?" he called out to the darkness. "What do you want?"

He knew perfectly well that whatever was lurking in his room would not answer him. It probably couldn't even understand his words.

Strange, unrelated thoughts raced across his mind, hindering his ability to focus on the dire situation he was in. His grandmother came into view in his head, her multi-colored apron flapping in the gentle breeze as she held out a dish stacked high with freshly baked cookies.

"Ricky dear, look, I've made some sweets for you."

He could practically still smell the chocolate chips.

Another vague memory of his grandmother filtered into his mind.

"Ricky dear, please help your old grandma. I need my teeth. They're in the glass in the bathroom."

Ricky shuddered when he thought about those nasty old teeth moldering away in their cleaning solution. How she put those things into her mouth he could never figure out.

"Ricky, are you there?"

The words weren't coming from some old memory he was reliving. These were coming from his room, from the shadow by the far wall.

"Ricky dear! Where are you boy?"

He swallowed hard and reached over to switch his lamp on. Predictably, nothing happened.

"Ricky?"

Feeling the need to arm himself, he began to search around the room for anything he could use as a weapon, finally settling for his old baseball bat.

The shadow was now emitting a low, nearly inaudible growl, which resonated off of the walls. Pictures rattled. A small glass fell to the ground. The light fixture above his bed swung back and forth.

"Ricky dear, help your old grandma."

A brief pause.

"Ricky dear, your old grandma misplaced her teeth again. Would you help me find them?"

Something shuffled in the darkness. Whatever it was it was having difficulty moving, struggling to gain control.

"Ricky! I know you're there! Just stay put and your old grandma will be right there."

Ricky closed his eyes and tightened his grip on the bat, trying desperately to hold on to the memories of his grandmother. In his mind his grandmother read bedtime stories to him. She baked him fresh chocolate chip cookies and played all of his favorite games with him, often letting him win. She did all of the typical things a loving grandmother did with her one and only grandson, including being there for him when his parents weren't.

But this wasn't his grandma. This thing that was slithering towards him in the supposed sanctuary of his bedroom on this chilly, crystal clear autumn night was not even human…at least not anymore.

"I'm coming Ricky dear," the thing drawled. "You just wait there for me…you hear me boy? You just wait for me."

Ricky began to impulsively play with his hair as he tried with all of his might to look away from the nightmare coming towards him. Should he call out to his parents for help? The overwhelming urge to do so was hard to resist, especially

68

considering the situation he was in, but his desire to prove that he wasn't a baby anymore to his strict and overbearing parents was also strong.

"Ricky dear, I'm coming. I'm almost there!"

"Mom! Dad! Help me! Mom? Dad?"

But the familiar sound of footsteps galloping down the hallway towards his room was alarmingly absent. Only the wet thuds of the thing approaching his bed filled the dark room. It slithered nearer and nearer to the bed, leaving a foul smelling residue in its wake. Ricky thanked Heaven that it was mostly hidden by the darkness.

"Ricky, I'm almost there." The words were followed by heavy grunting and slobbering. "And don't worry dear, your old grandma found her teeth this time. She's got them right where they belong…in my mouth!"

Ricky, spurred on by his instinct to survive, leaped out of his bed, and gripping the bat tightly in his sweaty hands, straightened up in front of the thing approaching.

More grunting and slobbering.

"Ricky dear, don't you want to see your old grandma?" The tone of the words had changed slightly, gravitating towards an elderly woman who was merely happy to see her grandson. It was still hidden by the darkness, only occasionally poking out a limb here or there, as if to stimulate its victim's imagination. It wanted Ricky to think about what it might look like, just what it might actually be.

Despite his fear Ricky found himself fascinated by the scenario unfolding before him. His imagination was running wild with possible explanations, each one trying to grasp plausible reasons for the horrible anomaly. He'd always had a strong and vivid imagination, it helped him to cope with the hardships in his life. His struggles in school, his general rejection from girls, the terrible voices that occasionally filled his head and… the death of his grandmother.

"Mom! Dad!"

Again no response.

The withered, bloodless hand of his dead grandmother slammed onto the floor, followed immediately by the other hand, revealing them from the darkness.

"Ricky dear, I'm right here. Your imagination has helped me so much. I'm coming. I'm coming."

Feeling the need for a better weapon, Ricky scanned the room for anything he could use. He wanted something bigger, something that wouldn't require him to get too close if he had to.

"Ricky? Ricky?"

Ricky jumped out of his bed and raced to the door, swinging it open in one swift motion. He suddenly remembered where he had left it, on the floor near the bathroom door, and if he could get to it in time it would prove to be just the ticket he needed.

To his great relief it was right where he had left it.

"Ricky, where'd you go?"

In a flash he was back in his bed brandishing his new weapon, reveling in the confidence it gave him.

The sunken corpse face emerged from the darkness. It was his grandmother, but not the one who used to bake him fresh chocolate chip cookies or let him win in
his favorite games. The face belonged in a cemetery, a horrific painting of death, fully intent on its foul purpose.

Ricky tightened his grip on the shovel as graveyard dirt cascaded down onto his bed. When he had exhumed his grandmother's remains the night before and brought them to the house he had no idea that his overactive imagination would go into overdrive like it did. He had only wanted her to be home again, to complete the family, just like it was before she had died. His parents were for the idea as well. Their bodies, which were decomposing in their bedroom, had told him so.

"Ricky? Ricky?"

His grandmother looked directly at him, her glassy eyes dripping down her gaunt face. He tried to look away but couldn't.

It was the price he had to pay for his actions, even though he did what he did for love.

But if it came to it would he have the strength to hit his own grandmother with a shovel? Could he bring himself to attack the very one he was trying so hard to bring back?

"There you are dear. Grandma's coming."

The carcass slithered up to the bed with remarkable agility, considering it had been under six feet of cold, hard dirt just a short while ago, and glared at Ricky with a stare of evil beyond comprehension. Ricky stared back, clinging to the thin belief that there was still a shred of humanity left in it, although he knew perfectly well there wasn't.

"G...Grandma? Is...is it really you?" The words stumbled out of his mouth, and he realized just how foolish they were. Of course it was his grandma. The tombstone had her name clearly etched on it. Plus he had recalled exactly where she had been buried. He remembered the funeral well.

Almost without thought he swung the shovel high over his head and slammed it down with all of his might onto his grandmother's rotting head. A sound like a ripe watermelon hitting concrete filled the room, followed immediately by a terrible stench, which clogged his senses with nausea. The corpse collapsed into an unrecognizable mass of decayed flesh. The shovel dropped to the floor as Ricky fell back into his bed, his mind racing with the implications of his actions.

Should he call the police? Would they believe him? How could he sleep with the dead body of his grandmother in his bedroom? Did he remember to turn the coffee pot off? Was ketchup on sale this week at the grocery store? And if it wasn't where could he get a good deal on some? He definitely needed some more ketchup.

He laid down on his bed, pulled the covers up to his chin and began to play with his hair. The silk trim on his blanket provided much needed comfort, just as it always had when he was a little kid, especially when he had to go to the doctors office

71

and get his medication. How he hated that place with all those nasty tests and needles.

He glanced over at the nightstand next to his bed. The small piece of paper with his doctor's messy signature scrawled on it reminded him that he had forgotten to get his prescription filled again. Not a problem though, he'd just have to remember to give it to his mom and she would take care of it like she always did.

"Mom?" he called out to the darkness. "Mom? I need my prescription filled. Mom?"

No response.

"Mom?"

Still no answer.

He looked across the room and was surprised to see the corpse of his grandmother. She was on her back and was completely intact. A thin layer of dirt covered most of her body and clogged her hair. Next to her was a small shovel, his shovel, which also had dirt on it.

"Mom? Dad? Grandma's still here. She's in my bedroom. Mom? Dad?"

The anxiety that he felt when he heard the familiar footsteps walking down the hallway towards his room was immense. But the fear that he felt when his bedroom door swung open was far, far worse.